The House of Hollow Graves: A Gothic Psychological Thriller Mystery

A HAUNTED HOUSE NOVEL FOR ADULTS—BLENDING GOTHIC HORROR FICTION, HISTORICAL GOTHIC HORROR, AND PSYCHOLOGICAL THRILLERS INTO AN UNFORGETTABLE DUAL TIMELINE MYSTERY (PSYCHOLOGICAL THRILLER FICTION BOOKS)

ROWAN HALE

CONTENTS

Untitled — v

Prologue — 1

PART ONE
THE INTERITANCE

1. The Letter — 5
2. Arrival — 8
3. First Night — 11
4. The Name in the Dust — 14
5. The Garden Wall — 18

PART TWO
THE UNFOLDING

6. Isadora's Journal — 25
7. Whispers & Footsteps — 29
8. The Locked Door — 35
9. The Room That Doesn't Exist — 41
10. Unwritten Things — 45
11. Flashback: Isadora (1892) — 50
12. The Séance Book — 55

PART THREE
DECENT

13. The Whispering Room — 63
14. Losing Time — 67
15. Flashback: Rituals — 72
16. The Ones Who Helped Bury Her — 77
17. Things That Shouldn't Change but Do — 81
18. The Place Where Names Go to Die — 86
19. The Last Trick of the House — 90

Epilogue – The House That Wasn't Silent Anymore — 94

AFTERWORD: From the Journal of Isadora Graves   99
Acknowledgments   101

Found tucked behind the dust jacket of a forgotten edition of Isadora's journal, dated 1892.

PROLOGUE

H*ollow Graves Manor, 1892*
POV: Isadora Graves
INT. UPPER BEDROOM – NIGHT
Wind moans through the broken panes. The wallpaper peels like dying skin.

ISADORA GRAVES, disheveled, wild-eyed, ink smudged on her fingers and across her white nightgown, crouches beside the fireplace. A flickering candle casts long shadows over the room's crumbling grandeur.

She's writing. Scratching words into the wall beneath the torn wallpaper—fast, frantic. The graphite tip of her pencil snaps. She doesn't stop.

Her breath hitches. A sound, distant at first—**a scraping, rhythmic drag**—rises from the floorboards. The walls tremble softly, almost... expectantly.

She stiffens.

ISADORA
(whispering)
Not yet. Please, not yet.

She shoves a yellowed paper into the spine of a hollowed-out book—*A Book of Natural Philosophy*. Her hands shake. The candle-light sputters as a **pressure** settles over the room, thick as fog.

INT. MIRROR – SIMULTANEOUS

The reflection ripples. In it, the room is *wrong*—the curtains blow in a wind that doesn't exist. A figure stands behind her: a woman in a high-necked black gown, eyes like tar pits, lips stitched shut.

Isadora doesn't look. Her voice breaks:

ISADORA
(to herself)
Do not look. Do not *see*.

The floor creaks outside the door.

She stumbles to the cradle in the corner—**empty**. She runs her hand over the blanket, the phantom warmth of something lost still lingering. Her face crumples—but there's no time for grief now.

The sound grows louder: something dragging its limbs up the basement stairs. A body too long, too heavy.

She crosses the room. The mirror pulses. The candle gutters. The **doorknob turns**—slowly.

ISADORA
(panicked whisper)
They live in the walls.

She carves it—**those five words**—into the plaster with a jagged piece of mirror. Her knuckles bleed.

The door creaks open.

A long shadow spills across the floor.

She doesn't scream.

She **blows out the candle.**

CUT TO BLACK.

SOUND: The house exhales. The whisper of dozens of voices, layered atop one another, echoing:

"They live in the walls."

PART ONE
THE INTERITANCE

CHAPTER 1
THE LETTER

Present Day – October
EXT. NEW ENGLAND COASTAL ROAD – DAY
A slate-gray sky hangs heavy over the winding two-lane road. Mist clings to the trees. The world feels like it's holding its breath.
INT. NORA'S CAR – CONTINUOUS
NORA BLACKWELL (29) grips the steering wheel with white-knuckled tension. She's dressed in layered flannel and fatigue, her tired eyes flicking between the cracked GPS screen and the rearview mirror. Her phone buzzes in the cupholder—ignored.
The houses grow further apart. Civilization thins.
She slows as a rusted iron gate looms ahead—overgrown, crooked, and hanging open like a broken jaw.
The sign reads:
Hollow Graves Manor
Private Property. Trespassers Will Be Prosecuted.
Nora stares at it. A beat. She exhales.
NORA
(to herself)

Right. Fresh start.

She drives through.

EXT. HOLLOW GRAVES MANOR – MOMENTS LATER

The mansion rises from the mist like a corpse dragged from the sea.

Tall, Victorian, **beautiful in its decay**—peeling paint, shattered windows, vines like veins climbing its frame. A tower leans ever so slightly, as if listening.

Nora parks.

Wind whips through the trees. The air feels… heavier here. Like stepping into someone else's memory.

She approaches the porch. The wood groans beneath her boots.

There's a key waiting in a rusted tin on the stoop, just like the lawyer promised. She unlocks the door.

INT. HOLLOW GRAVES MANOR – FOYER – CONTINUOUS

Darkness.

Dust hangs in the air like old breath.

The foyer unfolds in silence: a grand staircase draped in cobwebs, faded wallpaper curling at the seams, chandeliers dulled by time. The air smells of mildew and paper and something fainter… metallic.

She steps inside. The door creaks closed behind her.

SLAM.

She jumps. Whirls. The door is shut.

NORA
(calling out, nervous)
Hello?

Silence.

She moves deeper into the house. Her footsteps echo in a way that makes her feel **watched**.

In the parlor, a cracked mirror leans against the wall. She catches a glimpse of herself—

—and for a split second, swears there's **someone else** standing just behind her.

She turns. Nothing.

She shakes her head.

INT. UPSTAIRS HALLWAY – LATER

Nora carries a suitcase up the creaking staircase. The house *groans*, a low, shifting sound beneath her feet.

She pauses at the landing, breathing hard. Something whispers—so soft she thinks it's the wind.

But there's no breeze.

She follows the hallway to the **last door on the right**. Her assigned bedroom.

As she reaches for the knob, her fingers freeze.

There, just beside the doorframe—barely visible in the cracked paint—**words** have been etched into the wood, almost carved by fingernail:

Don't trust the door in the cellar.

A chill runs through her.

She touches the carving.

The house creaks again, deeper this time—like something shifting awake.

INT. NORA'S BEDROOM – NIGHT

She lies in bed, the old frame groaning with every breath she takes. A glass of wine sits untouched on the nightstand. Her phone is still dead.

Outside, the wind howls.

Inside, the house whispers.

And far below, from somewhere in the cellar—something begins to move.

CHAPTER 2
ARRIVAL

Moonlight slices through the cracked curtains. Shadows ripple against the faded wallpaper.

Nora sleeps fitfully, her arms curled tight against her chest. The old mattress groans beneath her with each shift, as if resisting rest.

A low **tick-tick-tick** echoes in the silence.

The wall clock? No.

It's coming from inside the wall.

HOLLOW GRAVES MANOR – PARLOR – NIGHT

Nora is no longer in bed.

She's standing barefoot in the parlor, wearing a long white nightdress that isn't hers. The furniture is **whole**, polished, freshly dusted. Candles burn in their sconces, flickering like they're gasping.

Music plays from the phonograph: a warbling lullaby that drifts in and out of tune.

A woman's laugh echoes faintly.

ISADORA (O.S.)

Tell me again, Doctor—what's the price of forgetting?

Nora turns. In the mirror, she catches a reflection that is not her own.

ISADORA, luminous and terrified, scribbles frantically on the wallpaper.

Nora moves toward her.

The paper peels away on its own. Beneath it, in frantic ink:

They're listening. Say nothing. Trust nothing.

Don't let them know you're awake.

Suddenly—**everything stops.**

The music. The candlelight. Even the air.

Then—

A sound from behind the walls.

Something **huge**, breathing.

The wallpaper **bulges**, as though something is pushing through from the other side.

Nora stumbles backward.

VOICE (WHISPERING, LAYERED)

Nora... Nora... Nora...

The house speaks her name in her own voice.

Then—

INT. NORA'S BEDROOM – MORNING

She jerks awake, soaked in sweat.

Silence.

Sunlight fights through the grime on the windows. The whispers are gone.

She exhales shakily and turns to sit up—then freezes.

There, on the nightstand, is a **book** that wasn't there the night before.

Old, leather-bound, spine cracked with age. *A Book of Natural Philosophy*.

Inside, tucked like a pressed flower, is a **torn journal page**, written in a slanted, looping hand.

It reads:

They've forgotten me. I pray you don't. If you can read this, you're already inside.

—*I.G.*

Nora stares.

From the hallway, a **single knock**.

Then silence.

CHAPTER 3
FIRST NIGHT

INT. HOLLOW GRAVES MANOR – PARLOR – NIGHT – 1892

The candles never stay lit for long anymore.

ISADORA GRAVES sits alone at the edge of the velvet settee, hands resting in her lap like folded paper. The fire crackles in the hearth, throwing copper light across the parlor's polished dark wood. Everything is *too quiet*, the kind of quiet that listens.

On the phonograph, a lullaby wobbles—an old nursery melody she barely remembers learning. She doesn't remember setting the needle.

The mirror across the room **ripples**.

She doesn't look at it.

The wallpaper on the far wall is curling at the edges, revealing the layers beneath—names, markings, warnings, all hers. All the versions of her that have lived through this nightmare in fragments.

A scratching noise begins behind her chair. Gentle at first. Curious.

She clenches her fists.

Not again. Not tonight.

. . .

INT. BASEMENT CORRIDOR – EARLIER

The air is cold and wet. Stone walls drip like the inside of a mouth.

Isadora moves carefully, holding a lantern close to her chest. Her nightgown trails against the floor. Bare feet on cold stone. The silence has weight here.

The door at the end—the iron one, rusted and bolted—is cracked open.

DR. GRAVES (O.S.), faint and muffled from beyond the door:

"The boundary is thinning. We are so close."

Isadora's breath catches.

She approaches slowly and peers through the gap.

Inside: an **altar**, circular markings on the floor, candles long since burned out. And at the center: a stained crib, empty but humming.

The shadows **move**—not as tricks of the light, but with *intention*.

She steps back. Something **smiles** from the dark.

INT. ISADORA'S STUDY – MOMENTS LATER

She slams the door shut behind her, locks it. The old phonograph starts playing again upstairs without being touched.

She grabs the mirror shard hidden inside the desk drawer, her hand shaking.

Scrapes it across the wallpaper. Again. Deeper. She must write it again.

They are not ghosts.
They are what's left after forgetting.
The walls feed them.

The whispering begins.

Low. Familiar.

VOICE (WHISPERING, LAYERED)

You called us. You called us. You called us.

ISADORA

I didn't mean to.

She crouches beside the fireplace, hiding her latest warning behind the soot-streaked bricks. Then she reaches for her locket, whispering the only name she still trusts.

ISADORA

Nora.

The flame in her lamp flickers—once. Twice.

The shadows along the walls begin to rise, stretch.

She knows they will come for her again soon.

But not tonight.

Tonight, she still remembers.

TRANSITION TO PRESENT: INT. NORA'S ROOM – MORNING

CLOSE ON: The torn journal page in Nora's hand, words written in the same looping hand:

I wrote this for you. I don't know how, but I remember your name.

Please don't forget mine.

— Isadora G.

Nora lowers the page, eyes wide.

The phonograph in the parlor—unplugged, unused—begins to play a lullaby.

CHAPTER 4
THE NAME IN THE DUST

EXT. ASHVALE HISTORICAL SOCIETY – LATE MORNING
The air smells like salt and woodsmoke. Ashvale looks like the kind of coastal town that forgot it existed after 1952—quaint antique shops, shuttered diners, peeling signs with names like **"The Silver Gull"** and **"Old World Remedies."**

Nora pushes open the door to the **Ashvale Historical Society**—a squat brick building with dusty windows and zero visitors.

Inside: **old paper**, **older books**, and the sound of a clock ticking too loudly.

INT. ARCHIVES ROOM – MOMENTS LATER
SIMON WARD looks up from behind a desk buried in microfilm reels and coffee-stained genealogy charts.

30s, tweed vest, the general air of a man who's spent more time with dead people than living ones.

He squints at Nora, then at the paper in her hand.

SIMON

Let me guess—you just inherited the *murder mansion*.
NORA
Hollow Graves?
SIMON
(sighs)
That's the one.

INT. HISTORICAL SOCIETY – RESEARCH AREA – LATER

They sit at a cluttered table.

Nora has unfolded the torn journal page she found in the night. She's not sure why she brought it—it feels intimate. Dangerous.

Simon pushes a faded blueprint across to her.

SIMON

Graves Manor was originally built in 1841. Reconstructed in 1889. There were rumors it was a convalescence home for women at one point—early mental health treatment, or what passed for it.

NORA

You mean an asylum.

SIMON

A discreet one. The kind that didn't show up in town records but buried people all the same.

He hesitates.

SIMON (CONT'D)

There's something else. People who go into that house don't always come out. A couple from Boston tried to renovate it ten years ago. She left. He didn't.

NORA

What happened to him?

SIMON

They found his boots on the porch. That's it.

. . .

Later that day, Nora returns to the house, heart still hammering from Simon's stories.

She walks the hall slowly, watching how the light shifts against the walls.

Dust motes drift like ash in the sunset.

She steps into one of the upper bedrooms she hasn't explored yet. It's cold here. **Too** cold.

The bed is made, untouched. A chair still faces the window.

And on the vanity mirror—drawn in the **fog of condensation**, though the room isn't warm enough for it—

Isadora.

She exhales shakily and turns back.

And freezes.

The hallway behind her has **changed**.

It's longer. Wrong.

The house is watching her.

INT. BASEMENT DOOR – NIGHT

Later, unable to sleep, she walks past the cellar door.

She swears—just as she passes—that she hears **breathing** behind it.

Not wind.

Breathing.

She runs her hand across the wood.

And sees something faintly scratched into the frame, nearly invisible in the dark:

Say nothing. Trust nothing.

INT. NORA'S BEDROOM – MIDNIGHT

She lies awake, the journal page under her pillow.

The phonograph plays again downstairs.

Same lullaby.
Same impossible sound.
She doesn't get up.
Not tonight.
She's starting to understand the rules.

CHAPTER 5
THE GARDEN WALL

EXT. HOLLOW GRAVES MANOR – GARDEN – MORNING

The overgrown garden is a tangle of ivy, thorns, and broken stone angels—forgotten beauty trying to claw its way back to the surface.

Nora pushes through the underbrush in borrowed gloves, clearing branches until she reaches a **wall** made of ancient stone. Not part of the manor's fencing. Older.

Built like it was meant to **keep something in**, not out.

Faint carvings line the base. Worn symbols. Circles intersected by eyes, triangles with bleeding edges. One of them glows faintly **when she touches it**—just for a second.

She stumbles back, heart hammering.

INT. ASHVALE HISTORICAL SOCIETY – LATER

Nora arrives with a sketch of the symbol. **Simon** greets her with his usual sardonic half-smile, but this time it falters when he sees what she's brought.

SIMON
Where did you find this?

NORA
Stone wall behind the house. Looked like a boundary line. Why?

Simon hesitates. Runs a finger over the symbol.

SIMON
This… this is old. Not Graves old. Older than the house. Local folklore calls it a "binding mark." Supposedly seals things beneath the soil.

NORA
Like… a grave?

SIMON
(grim)
Or something that shouldn't have been dug up in the first place.

INT. HISTORICAL SOCIETY – LATER

They sit side-by-side on the worn leather bench, poring over a crumbling town ledger.

Nora watches Simon's hands as he flips through pages. Steady. Focused. But there's a tension in his jaw he's trying to hide.

NORA
You don't believe in any of this… do you?

SIMON
I believe the house kills people. I don't know *how*. And maybe that's worse.

He looks up at her.

SIMON (CONT'D)
People disappear. Or they come out broken. But you? You don't seem like someone who scares easy.

NORA

(scoffs)
I'm terrified. I just don't have anywhere else to go.
That lands heavier than she means it to.
A quiet beat.
SIMON
If it gets bad—really bad—you leave. No matter what you find. No matter what it wants to show you.
NORA
I can't. Not yet.

Nora walks back from town under a sky that looks like spilled ink. The house waits at the end of the road like a patient monster.

She stops at the garden again. Looks at the wall.

Something's been **dug up** beside it—fresh, loose earth she doesn't remember seeing that morning.

There are footprints in the dirt. Bare.

Her own size.

HOLLOW GRAVES – LIBRARY – LATER

She curls into a faded leather chair with Simon's copied notes. Her fingers trail over one line:

The house was never empty. It only pretended to sleep.

Lightning flashes. The chandelier above her swings—once.

And far beneath the house, **something shifts**.

SIMON'S APARTMENT – SAME NIGHT

Simon sits at his desk, staring at an old photograph.

The **original staff photo** from the manor.

In the back row: a man who looks exactly like Simon.

His name has been scratched out.

He runs a hand through his hair.
SIMON
(softly)
What did you do?
He doesn't sleep that night.

PART TWO
THE UNFOLDING

CHAPTER 6
ISADORA'S JOURNAL

HOLLOW GRAVES MANOR – LIBRARY – MORNING

Rain taps against the stained-glass windows like fingernails.

Nora sits curled in the leather chair, the fire low, a blanket around her shoulders. The book Simon gave her lies open in her lap—pages filled with clipped newspaper articles and faded photographs of Hollow Graves.

She flips to a page pressed flat with old tape. An image of **Isadora Graves**.

Hair pinned high. Corset drawn too tight. Eyes that look straight through the lens.

NORA
(softly)
Who were you?

Thunder cracks outside. The fire pops.

From the shelf behind her—**a book falls.**

She jumps. The room is still.

The book lies open on the carpet, spine cracked. Not from the collection she touched.

Inside: a **loose journal page**, curled at the edges, hidden between the pages of *Jane Eyre*.

She picks it up.

He feeds them to the house. The women. The ones no one misses. And it keeps them. Their voices. Their faces. Their names.

But the house cannot lie forever.

HOLLOW GRAVES – UPSTAIRS HALLWAY – LATER

She walks the hall slowly, trailing her fingers along the faded wallpaper.

She passes the **whispering room** again—the one she hasn't opened.

She stops.

From inside, she hears her name. Soft. Sweet.

NORA (O.S.)

Nora... come in. I want to show you something.

She stiffens. That voice—it's *hers*.

Exactly her voice.

She backs away.

The doorknob jiggles.

NORA (O.S.)

I'm not going to hurt you.

She runs.

INT. FOYER – MOMENTS LATER

Nora stumbles down the stairs, heart racing, breath ragged.

Simon stands at the bottom, soaked from the rain, holding a thermos and a bag of books.

SIMON

...did I miss something?

NORA

(quietly)

The house used my voice.

Simon's expression hardens.

INT. DINING ROOM – AFTERNOON

They sit across from each other. Books open. Candle burning. Thunder rolling.

NORA

It wasn't just a mimic. It knew things I'd said before. In my exact tone. Same pause. Same rhythm. Like it... *recorded* me.

SIMON

Or it *is* you. A version of you.

He taps a journal.

SIMON (CONT'D)

These houses—especially ones tied to trauma—have a history of echoing emotional imprints. Psychic residue. Like... replaying grief on a loop.

NORA

But it's not on a loop. It talks *back*.

INT. PARLOR – EVENING

The storm quiets.

Simon helps her move a bookshelf to access a warped doorway. Behind it: a **sealed door**, rusted and swollen shut.

They sit beside it, catching their breath.

A long pause.

SIMON

Why'd you stay, Nora?

NORA

No one else wanted me to. And... the house did.

He looks at her.

SIMON

You know that's not comforting, right?

NORA

It's not meant to be.

Another silence.

Then—her voice again. **From behind the sealed door.**

NORA (O.S.)

Simon... let me out.

His eyes widen.

SIMON

That's not funny.

NORA

I didn't say anything.

They both stare at the door.

CHAPTER 7
WHISPERS & FOOTSTEPS

HOLLOW GRAVES MANOR – LIBRARY – LATE NIGHT
Rain has stopped. The fire is low. Outside, fog curls around the trees like breath.

Nora and Simon sit on the floor beside the hearth, the last candle between them guttering low. Half-empty mugs of tea sit on stacked books. The silence is companionable but heavy—like a question waiting to be asked.

Simon breaks it.

SIMON

Did you ever believe in ghosts? Before this.

Nora wraps the blanket tighter around her.

NORA

I believed in forgetting. In pretending. Same thing, right?

He doesn't push. Just waits.

NORA (CONT'D)

My mother never talked about her side of the family. Not once. The only time she got close, she told me some people... aren't meant to be remembered. That they were better left buried.

She meets his eyes.

NORA (CONT'D)
Now I'm living in their house.
A soft, bitter laugh.
SIMON
My dad used to keep records of every family in Ashvale. Obsessive stuff—births, deaths, property lines. He had boxes marked with names I didn't recognize. But Hollow Graves... he never touched it. Like it was *taboo*.
He looks down at his hands.
SIMON (CONT'D)
Found one of those boxes last year. Name scratched off. Photos. Letters. A man who looks exactly like me, standing behind Elijah Graves.
NORA
You think you're related to them?
SIMON
I know I am. I just don't know what that means yet.
A long pause.
The fire crackles. The house creaks.
NORA
Maybe that's why we're both here. Not just to uncover what happened—but to decide what *doesn't* get buried again.
Simon looks at her—something unspoken flickering in his expression. Not romance yet, but **recognition**. The kind you only give someone who knows the weight of memory.
He nods.
SIMON
Then let's find the truth. Together.

ASHVALE HISTORICAL SOCIETY – NEXT DAY
The archive room smells like dust and something colder.
Nora flips through brittle newspaper clippings while Simon rolls microfilm reels with one hand and scribbles in a notebook with the other.

On the table between them: a photograph of the **Graves family**—Elijah, Isadora, and two women Nora doesn't recognize. None of them smile.

SIMON

Officially, the family left Ashvale in 1893. No forwarding address. No sales records. No letters.

NORA

So they just vanished?

SIMON

Vanished… or were disappeared.

He slides a birth certificate toward her.

SIMON (CONT'D)

Look. Patient records from 1892—sanatorium wing. Most of them only list initials. But this one?

NORA

I.G.

SIMON

Isadora Graves. She wasn't staff. She was a patient.

Nora stares at the name, heart stuttering.

NORA

She committed herself?

SIMON

Or was committed.

He turns the page. A single line in a doctor's handwriting:

Subject exhibits delusions of inherited memory. Claims future generations will hear her voice.

Nora goes cold.

HOLLOW GRAVES MANOR – ATTIC – NIGHT

Nora follows Simon into the attic. It smells of moths, dry rot, and cedar.

They dig through crates until she finds it: a velvet box containing a **silver locket**, warm to the touch.

Inside, a photograph—Isadora, alone. Behind her, on the wall, someone has carved a message barely visible in the shadows of the image:

If you can read this, you're already inside.

Simon shines his flashlight on the locket.

SIMON
You feel that?

NORA
It's humming.

The moment is shattered—**a crash below**. Something falls in the parlor.

They freeze.

SIMON
That wasn't the wind.

PARLOR – MOMENTS LATER

They descend the stairs together.

The mirror has fallen, shattered across the floor.

The fireplace is lit.

Neither of them started it.

In the flames: a page, curling to ash before they can read it. But one word stands out, just before it burns:

Return.

HOLLOW GRAVES – PARLOR – AFTERNOON (FLASHBACK)

ISADORA sits by the fire, dressed in pale silk. Her hands are folded in her lap, trembling slightly, though she holds her posture like a statue.

Across from her, **DR. ELIJAH GRAVES**, her husband, pours tea as if this were any ordinary afternoon.

ISADORA
You've locked the west wing.

ELIJAH

For repairs.

ISADORA

I know what you keep in that wing. I heard the screams.

He smiles without warmth.

ELIJAH

Delusions, my dear, are not facts. You've been unwell for weeks. Ever since the miscarriage.

Isadora flinches. Her teacup clinks against the saucer.

ISADORA

The house whispered to me before that. Before the blood. Before the cradle went quiet.

Elijah sits across from her. Leans in.

ELIJAH

It's grief. You're unmoored. You're making connections where none exist. Just like your mother did, before—

He doesn't finish.

ISADORA

So you'll lock me up, too?

INT. HOLLOW GRAVES – SECOND FLOOR – NIGHT

Isadora is escorted by **two silent attendants** into a locked bedroom. The door bolts behind her.

The wallpaper is the same floral pattern she once chose herself. It now feels like it's watching her.

She bangs the door.

ISADORA

You can't silence me. I remember what you did.

No answer. Just footsteps, retreating.

She sinks to the floor, sobbing—until the fireplace crackles.

She didn't light it.

From inside the flames, a whisper:

Write it down.

She looks around, wide-eyed. Slowly, she rises, pulls a pencil from her vanity, and walks to the wall.

She peels back the wallpaper and begins to write.

If I forget, it wins. If I stay silent, it feeds.

They are in the walls. He gave them names, then took their voices.

A cold wind brushes her cheek.

She turns.

In the mirror: **a dozen pale figures** stand behind her. Eyes sewn shut. Mouths open, but silent.

Only Isadora can hear them scream.

CHAPTER 8
THE LOCKED DOOR

The house was breathing again.

Not in the way that made floorboards groan or the old pipes sigh—not the charming, creaky kind of life that old buildings held—but something deeper, more deliberate. Like the entire structure was drawing breath into its rotted bones and holding it, waiting for her to notice.

Nora stood in the kitchen just after midnight, barefoot on the cool black-and-white tile, staring at the cellar door.

She hadn't planned to come down here. In truth, she hadn't *walked* here. One moment she was in bed, wide awake but still—listening to the wind howl across the eaves—and the next, she was in the kitchen, fingers hovering inches from the doorknob.

The door had been locked for weeks. She'd checked it that first night, rattled it out of curiosity, then promptly moved on. A heavy iron latch barred it from the outside, as though someone long ago wanted to keep something **in**.

Now, the latch hung crooked. **Unlatched.**

She didn't remember opening it.

The air near the door felt strange—*thicker*, like the way humidity presses down before a thunderstorm. Except it was warm. Radiating heat that pulsed against her skin like the slow throb of a fever.

Nora took a step closer.

The house fell quiet, as if holding its breath with her.

Then—

A sound from the other side of the door.

Knock.

Three taps.

Deliberate. Evenly spaced.

She froze. Her heart lurched, stalling in her chest like an engine choking on silence.

Then—again:

Knock. Knock. Knock.

The same rhythm. Like an answer.

Nora backed away.

"Nope," she whispered to no one.

But she didn't run. Couldn't. Her legs felt filled with wet sand, her limbs bound by invisible thread. Something wanted her to listen.

She stepped forward again. Slowly. One pace. Then another.

She pressed her palm against the door.

And heard her voice.

"Let me out."

Not a whisper. Not faint. It was her own voice, exactly. Calm. Familiar. Just on the other side of the wood.

She recoiled like she'd been burned, stumbling backward into the table. A knife clattered to the floor, slicing through the silence like a scream.

The house groaned in response. A long, low creak that wasn't from the walls or the floor but from *something deeper*, beneath the foundation.

It was waking up.

SHE RAN.

Not up the stairs. Not at first. Her body fought itself, every instinct pulling in a different direction. But eventually, her feet obeyed the terror blooming in her chest, and she fled through the hallway, past the parlor, past the library, up the wide, groaning stairs.

At the landing, she stopped, gripping the railing hard enough that her knuckles paled.

From below, she heard it.

Her own voice again.

"Nora."

Soft. Sweet. Familiar.

"Let me in."

She didn't answer.

NORA'S BEDROOM – LATER

She sat on the edge of the bed, Isadora's journal open in her lap, though she wasn't reading.

The house had gone still again. But the silence was worse than the sound.

On the floor near the door, she'd pushed a chair against the handle. A useless gesture, probably, but it gave her the illusion of control. She held the silver locket in her hand, thumb tracing the cold filigree edge over and over again.

It was cold. Ice cold. But when she held it, the whispers seemed to fade.

On the page beneath her fingers, Isadora's writing looped across the yellowed paper:

The door lies. But it must be opened eventually.

When it calls you in your own voice, do not answer. That is when it has learned your name.

Nora blinked, her throat dry.

A gust of wind rattled the windows.

Then—
Creak.
The cellar door opened.
She knew it before she heard it fully. The sound of wood dragging across tile. The slow release of a groaning hinge that hadn't moved in years.

Footsteps followed.

Not heavy. Not dragging. Just light, bare, padding footsteps, one after the other, slow and sure, crossing the kitchen floor.

Then the parlor.

Then the hall.

Then—

Outside her bedroom door.

They stopped.

A moment passed. Long. Breathless.

Then came the knock.

One. Soft. Knock.

She didn't move.

Didn't breathe.

Didn't blink.

She curled her fingers tighter around the locket, whispered Isadora's name.

The knock didn't come again.

But her voice did.

NORA (O.S.)

I know you're awake.

And then—

Silence.

Not just in the hallway.

But in the whole house.

A silence so deep it felt like being buried alive.

She sat there for hours.

The candle burned low beside her. The locket remained cold.

She didn't sleep.

And when dawn broke, pale and quiet, Nora rose to her feet.

She would not run.

She would not hide.

She would **not be silenced.**

Today, she would find out what waited behind the cellar door.

Binding Instructions—
Amendment V

Do not speak the name
unless you intend to finish it.

Do not let it learn your grief.

If it asks to be remembered,
say the name.

But if it offers to forget…
run.

CHAPTER 9
THE ROOM THAT DOESN'T EXIST

The house did not sleep in the daytime.
    It only **pretended** to.
    Nora knew that now.

HOLLOW GRAVES MANOR – UPSTAIRS HALLWAY – MIDDAY

Sunlight filters through the stained-glass window at the end of the hall, casting fractured colors across the warped floorboards. It would almost be beautiful, if the house didn't feel like it was watching her.

She's been tracing her steps—pacing the upstairs like a looped memory—until she finds it.

The mirror.

She'd passed it a dozen times since moving in: a full-length Victorian relic mounted to the wall just across from the master bedroom. She'd seen herself in it. Brushed her teeth in its reflection. Checked her bruised eyes after restless nights.

But today... something is different.

The mirror is **fogged**.

Not just cloudy—**breathing**. As though someone has exhaled onto the glass from the inside.

She lifts a hand, traces her fingers across the surface—and freezes.

The glass ripples. Just slightly. Like water.

Then she notices it.

At the base of the frame: a seam. Barely visible. A vertical line where the wall has been plastered over. Hidden. **Sealed.**

A hidden door.

The mirror isn't just a fixture.

It's an entrance.

HIDDEN ROOM – MOMENTS LATER

It takes force—prying with a fire iron, her shoulder, curses under her breath—but finally the panel gives way with a **groan**, and behind it: darkness.

A room.

A small one.

Not on the blueprints.

She ducks inside.

Dust fills her lungs immediately. She coughs, covering her mouth, her flashlight beam cutting through the stillness like a blade.

The room smells like **old paper** and **salt**.

There's a **writing desk** against one wall, drawers hanging open. A candle, melted into a pool on a brass plate. The bed is narrow, unmade. The sheets are yellowed, brittle with age.

Everything untouched. As if someone locked the door and *forgot the person inside ever existed.*

HIDDEN ROOM – CONTINUOUS

Nora walks slowly, every step crunching broken glass underfoot.

She finds:

- A broken hair comb.
- A child's music box, silent.
- A torn chemise, bloodstained at the collar.
- A journal—**Isadora's**.

She opens it.

Inside, the ink is blotched and erratic. The handwriting grows more frantic, more slanted, more fragmented with each entry.

He lied. The ritual was never to seal it. He fed them to it. One by one.

He said I would be the anchor. The voice.

But it wants more. It remembers. It listens through the walls.

It has learned to mimic the living.

She flips to the final entry:

If you've found this, you're part of it now.

Do not let it rewrite you. It knows your grief. It will use your guilt.

Beneath the mirror is the seal. Break it—and the truth will find light again.

Burn it if you must. But do not believe its promises.

Nora lowers the journal.

And that's when she hears it:

Breathing.

Not hers.

Behind her.

She turns slowly.

In the corner of the room, where shadow pools thickest, stands a **woman-shaped figure**—barely distinguishable from the dark, but *there*. Watching.

Not moving.

Not blinking.

A mirror of a mirror.

Nora stumbles back out the doorway, slamming it shut behind her.

UPSTAIRS HALLWAY – MOMENTS LATER

She stares at the mirror, heart racing.

It shows only her.

Only her.

But for a moment—just as she turns away—it ripples again.

LIBRARY – NIGHT

Later, Nora lays the journal open across the floor, tracing Isadora's final words. She lights a fire, not because she's cold, but because the house **feels closer** tonight.

The locket is warm again.

She whispers to it:

NORA

I won't let you be forgotten.

And this time—

She hears a whisper back.

Faint. Grateful. Distant.

ISADORA (O.S.)

Then it won't win.

CHAPTER 10
UNWRITTEN THINGS

The house had stopped pretending.

That was the first thing she noticed when she woke up on the parlor couch, wrapped in her grandmother's faded quilt.

She blinked into the soft amber light, the last embers of the fire sighing into stillness. Everything looked as it should—but *felt* as if it had shifted two inches to the left. Like waking up in someone else's memory of the same room.

Her mouth tasted of smoke and something bitter.

She did not remember falling asleep here.

Nora sat up slowly.

On the table before her sat a porcelain teacup filled with steaming liquid—still warm, still untouched. She hadn't made tea. She hadn't even boiled water.

Beside the cup sat her journal.

Open.

But not to the last page she had written.

The handwriting was hers. The pen marks. The ink. The way the lowercase **g** always looped too wide, the awkward slant of her **t's**.

But the words were not.
The house is a home. The home is a heart. The heart must be fed.

She slammed the journal shut so hard it shook the tea cup.

Her breath stuttered.

This wasn't paranoia. This wasn't sleepwalking.

The house was writing inside her.

BATHROOM – MOMENTS LATER

She stared at herself in the mirror.

Eyes sunken. Pupils wide. Skin pale beneath her freckles. But it was still her, wasn't it?

She lifted her shirt.

Four thin scratches lined her side, just under her ribs—angry red marks like thorn scratches. She hadn't noticed them last night.

She hadn't noticed **a lot of things** lately.

LIBRARY – MID-MORNING

She tried to ground herself. Fire in the hearth. A notebook open. Pages of Isadora's journal beside her.

It didn't help.

Every time she looked away from the notebook, she found new words written when she looked back. Nothing overt. Just small additions. A phrase here. A word there.

Always whispering the same message:

Let go. Let go. Let go.

She tore out the page. Burned it.

The fire popped, like it laughed at her.

NORA'S BEDROOM – LATER

She texted Simon. Twice.

NORA: *Are you okay?*

NORA: *Please call me.*

No response.

She left a voicemail. Heard her voice tremble. Hated it.

She thought about walking to town, but the fog outside was too thick, too dense, curling against the windows like the fingers of a dreaming beast.

It wasn't safe.

PARLOR – AFTERNOON

She sat on the floor, surrounded by books, staring into the cold hearth. Her thoughts drifted to the rumors Simon had shared about the previous owners. The ones who'd gone missing. The ones who left everything behind, as if the house had **devoured time around them.**

Her gaze fell to the hearthstone. Just one, slightly discolored, cracked down the middle like a split tooth.

Something called to her from beneath it.

Not a voice. A **pressure**. An idea. Not her own.

She stood.

FIREPLACE – MOMENTS LATER

Nora pried up the hearthstone with the fireplace poker, breath shallow.

It gave with a groan of age and grit, revealing a hollow space filled with dust and bone-dry air. Inside: a bundle wrapped in oilcloth.

She pulled it out with trembling hands.

The cloth unfurled to reveal:

- A child's porcelain doll, face singed

- A lock of dark brown hair, braided and tied with ribbon
- And a single brittle page—folded with exquisite care

She unfolded it.

A ritual. Not folklore. Not theory.

Instructions.

To bind what lives beneath: the blood of the last, the breath of the willing, and the name that breaks the silence.

— E. Graves, April 18, 1892

The date. The same day Isadora vanished.

She stared at the page.

The fire behind her sputtered to life.

She hadn't lit it.

LIBRARY – NIGHT

She paced.

Had she already been rewritten?

Had the house already slipped into her skin like smoke and claimed her fingers, her voice, her pen?

She thought about the mirror. The voice behind the cellar door. The journal entries she didn't write. The way her memory skipped and stitched itself together only after she checked the clocks.

The house wasn't haunting her anymore.

It was **remaking her**.

PARLOR – LATE NIGHT

She sat by the fire, wrapped in the same quilt, but no longer comforted.

She whispered Simon's name.

Once. Twice.

No reply.

Then—from the flames:

SIMON (O.S.)

Nora... come down here.

She froze.

The voice was his. **Exactly his**. No static, no echo. The exact tone he used when teasing her, when asking for help with something too heavy for one person.

SIMON (O.S.)

I found the truth. You need to see it.

A pause.

SIMON (O.S.)

I'm just past the door.

Her hands curled into fists.

Because she **wanted** to believe it. More than anything.

But something deeper inside—maybe hers, maybe Isadora's—whispered:

He never made it back to town.

That isn't him.

Not anymore.

She stood.

But she didn't move toward the door.

CHAPTER II
FLASHBACK: ISADORA (1892)

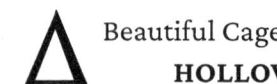

A Beautiful Cage

HOLLOW GRAVES MANOR – CONVALESCENT WING – NIGHT

There was a time when Isadora loved this house.

Before the silence crept in. Before the walls began to hum. Before the cellar door groaned in her dreams.

Before Elijah lied.

Now, she sat in a high-backed chair inside a room she no longer recognized—though it bore her name on the medical records nailed to the outside:

Patient: I. Graves, 34 – Female hysteria, delusional ideation

The windows had been nailed shut. The doors only opened from the outside.

The wallpaper still bore the florals she chose herself. Peonies. Now faded and curling like dead petals.

ISADORA
(to herself, quietly)
They're keeping me like a painting. Beautiful. Silent. Hung in a gilded frame.

She clutched her journal to her chest. It had taken three days of pretending to sleep, pretending not to hear them, pretending to forget… just to steal the pencil.

She pressed it to the inside flap.

He thinks I've forgotten.

He thinks he's broken me.

He doesn't know the house told me what he's done.

It showed me the other women. The ones he called patients. The ones who never left.

She heard footsteps outside the door. She stilled, eyes on the keyhole.

Not Elijah.

The attendant. One of his hired men. Hired silence.

She waited until the steps faded, then rose.

The floor groaned beneath her, a sound like a creature stretching its limbs after a long sleep.

SECOND FLOOR – SECRET CORRIDOR – MOMENTS LATER

By candlelight, Isadora crept behind the bookshelves of the library—through a corridor only she knew, once used by servants. It wrapped the house like a spine.

She came to a wall.

Knelt.

Scraped away a piece of molding with her nails.

Behind it, tucked into the space between beams: **a set of folded papers.**

Elijah's handwriting.

The ritual.

To seal the space between worlds, a conduit must be chosen.

She must know the pain of loss. She must speak the name forgotten. She must give herself willingly.

And scribbled beside it:

I. Graves – viable.

BASEMENT – THAT NIGHT

She lit her own way. Not with oil or with faith—but with the clarity of betrayal.

The cellar smelled of iron, mildew, and blood long since dried.

At the center of the chamber: a circle burned into the stone. Charred wax pooled in six points like clock ticks. Symbols marked the walls—some written in ink, some in ash, one in something darker.

The crib sat in the corner.

Empty.

She moved toward it.

Inside: a lock of her hair.

A bundle of her letters.

A strip of her nightdress.

A shrine.

To **her.**

He'd been planning it for months. Perhaps longer.

The walls trembled. Something shifted behind the brick.

She felt it watching her.

ISADORA

I am not yours to offer.

She picked up a shard of mirror from the floor—one she had shattered the week before.

She held it to her chest.

ISADORA (CONT'D)

But if I must be the anchor, I will not be the chain.

She carved a sigil into the stone. Her own.

A reversal of his ritual.

Blood trickled down her palm as she pressed it into the center.

A name must be spoken. A truth must be known. A voice must not be silenced.

She whispered her name into the circle.

ISADORA

Isadora Graves.

The candles flared. The walls screamed.

And then—

Darkness.

SEALED ROOM – MOMENTS LATER

She woke hours—or seconds—later, in the hidden room behind the mirror.

The door had been sealed shut.

The walls were quiet now.

Too quiet.

The house had taken something from her.

But not everything.

She would leave **words behind**.

She would carve them in cracks, in book spines, in the dust behind mirrors and inside the mouths of dolls.

Because the house remembers the silent—but it cannot forget the written.

CHAPTER 12
THE SÉANCE BOOK

The house had learned to whisper.

Now, it was learning to **bend.**

Nora felt it in small ways at first—misplaced objects, lights flickering in the corner of her vision, clocks ticking out of sync. But the attic... the attic would be different.

She knew that even before she climbed the narrow, groaning staircase with Simon at her back.

HOLLOW GRAVES – ATTIC STAIRCASE – AFTERNOON

The attic door was sealed with a rusted chain and a padlock that looked older than both of them. Simon fiddled with it, then pulled a hairpin from his coat.

NORA

Where'd you learn that?

SIMON

Ashvale has very few hobbies and far too many antique locks.

The lock snapped open.

As Simon pulled the chain free, the temperature dropped sharply.

The air rushed past them, smelling of cedar, ash, and something like lavender left too long in a drawer.

The door creaked open slowly.

ATTIC – MOMENTS LATER

The attic was larger than Nora expected.

It unfolded like a cathedral of rot—high rafters latticed with cobwebs, trunks and broken furniture draped in dusty sheets. Shafts of dim light pierced through cracks in the roof, illuminating particles of dust that danced like ash in still air.

The silence wasn't silence.

It was **waiting**.

NORA

It feels... heavier up here.

SIMON

It's the pressure. This part of the house has been sealed since the '30s.

They moved carefully through the maze of forgotten things. A rocking horse with a missing eye. A wedding dress, yellowed with age. A dollhouse that looked **exactly like the manor**.

Nora stopped.

NORA

Look.

Beneath a sheet, a small round table. Candles melted down to the base. A stack of papers. And at the center—an open book with **black leather binding**, cracked and curling.

The title had been burned into the cover:

SPIRITVS: A Guide to Communion and Conduction

Simon picked it up with both hands, reverently, like a priest lifting a holy text.

ATTIC – READING THE BOOK – LATER

The book was written in multiple hands—some elegant, others scrawled. Some in English, others in Latin. The margins were full of annotations in faded red ink.

Do not speak the third name aloud.

If the spirit mimics your voice, you are already within the veil.

The house is not a portal. It is the vessel.

Nora flipped to a page marked with a red ribbon.

The diagram was a **ritual circle**, with symbols she'd seen on the garden wall. One phrase had been underlined three times:

The hollow must be named to be bound.

SIMON

This isn't about talking to spirits. This is about **feeding** them. Containing them.

He pulled out a folded page tucked inside the back cover.

A name written in shaky ink:

Isadora Graves

Attempted binding failed. Conduit too strong. House adapted.

ATTIC – DISTORTION BEGINS

Suddenly, the light shifted.

Outside, the sky had been pale. Now it burned orange—sunset? No. Not possible. They hadn't been up here that long.

NORA

Simon... how long have we been reading?

Simon checked his watch. Frowned. Tapped the face.

SIMON

It says an hour. But... it was just after noon. Wasn't it?

They turned.

The doorway behind them was gone.

In its place: another wall. Seamless.

Nora reached out. Touched it.

Solid.

The attic had closed them in.

SIMON

This isn't right.

The shadows shifted again.

And something moved in the rafters above.

Not rats. Not birds.

Footsteps.

Light ones.

Bare.

They turned slowly.

At the far end of the attic, a figure stood.

A child.

Pale. Hair matted. Eyes empty.

She pointed at Nora.

Opened her mouth.

NORA (O.S.)

Help me.

The voice was Nora's.

The child opened her mouth again—**too wide**—and black smoke spilled out.

Nora and Simon backed away, heartbeats thunderous in their ears.

SIMON

Go. Move. Now.

They ran, weaving through old furniture and broken memories until the wall **opened** again, like a curtain lifting. They tumbled through the doorway.

SECOND FLOOR LANDING – MOMENTS LATER

They slammed the attic door shut.

Nora's knees buckled. She pressed her back against the wall, gasping.

NORA

ATTIC – READING THE BOOK – LATER

The book was written in multiple hands—some elegant, others scrawled. Some in English, others in Latin. The margins were full of annotations in faded red ink.

Do not speak the third name aloud.

If the spirit mimics your voice, you are already within the veil.

The house is not a portal. It is the vessel.

Nora flipped to a page marked with a red ribbon.

The diagram was a **ritual circle**, with symbols she'd seen on the garden wall. One phrase had been underlined three times:

The hollow must be named to be bound.

SIMON

This isn't about talking to spirits. This is about **feeding** them. Containing them.

He pulled out a folded page tucked inside the back cover.

A name written in shaky ink:

Isadora Graves

Attempted binding failed. Conduit too strong. House adapted.

ATTIC – DISTORTION BEGINS

Suddenly, the light shifted.

Outside, the sky had been pale. Now it burned orange—sunset? No. Not possible. They hadn't been up here that long.

NORA

Simon... how long have we been reading?

Simon checked his watch. Frowned. Tapped the face.

SIMON

It says an hour. But... it was just after noon. Wasn't it?

They turned.

The doorway behind them was gone.

In its place: another wall. Seamless.

Nora reached out. Touched it.

Solid.

The attic had closed them in.

SIMON

This isn't right.

The shadows shifted again.

And something moved in the rafters above.

Not rats. Not birds.

Footsteps.

Light ones.

Bare.

They turned slowly.

At the far end of the attic, a figure stood.

A child.

Pale. Hair matted. Eyes empty.

She pointed at Nora.

Opened her mouth.

NORA (O.S.)

Help me.

The voice was Nora's.

The child opened her mouth again—**too wide**—and black smoke spilled out.

Nora and Simon backed away, heartbeats thunderous in their ears.

SIMON

Go. Move. Now.

They ran, weaving through old furniture and broken memories until the wall **opened** again, like a curtain lifting. They tumbled through the doorway.

SECOND FLOOR LANDING – MOMENTS LATER

They slammed the attic door shut.

Nora's knees buckled. She pressed her back against the wall, gasping.

NORA

It used me. It used my voice again.

SIMON

It didn't just use it. It **wore** it.

He looked down at the séance book in his hands. Clutched it like a weapon.

SIMON (CONT'D)

This is a manual. Not to contact the dead. To **seal** them. Or something worse.

He flipped to the back cover. Scribbled there in the final page:

This house is not haunted.

It is haunting.

And it is hungry.

PARLOR – NIGHT

They sat in silence.

The fireplace crackled, but neither of them moved to feed it.

Nora stared at the firelight, Isadora's journal in one hand, the séance book in the other.

Outside, wind clawed at the shutters.

And upstairs, in the attic they had just escaped, something laughed.

It sounded like **both of them.**

PART THREE
DECENT

CHAPTER 13
THE WHISPERING ROOM

Some rooms don't have secrets.
They **are** the secret.
And Nora was standing in front of one.

SECOND FLOOR – WHISPERING ROOM DOOR – NIGHT
The door had always been there.
Tucked at the far end of the hall, painted the same dull ivory as every other. It had never drawn attention to itself. It wasn't grand. It wasn't locked.
It was **quiet**.
Until now.
Tonight, as the wind howled outside and thunder trembled against the old bones of Hollow Graves, **the door whispered**.
Faint and layered.
Hundreds of voices speaking at once. Some murmuring. Some sobbing. One—sounding like a **child**—laughing.
And woven among them all... **her own voice**, soft and urgent:
NORA (O.S.)

Don't open it. Please. Not yet.
Nora stood with her hand on the doorknob.
And turned it anyway.

THE WHISPERING ROOM – CONTINUOUS
Darkness swallowed her instantly.
No windows. No light. Only the shallow glow of her flashlight, flickering like it wanted to go out.
The air was still. Too still. Not just quiet—**deafeningly quiet**, like the air had been thickened by something she couldn't see.
The room was small. Square. Empty—at first glance.
But when she turned in a slow circle, she saw them.
The walls were covered in names.
Hundreds. Thousands.
Carved, scratched, gouged.
Some shallow. Some deep.
All of them **women's names**.
All of them ending in silence.
She ran her fingers across a few:
E. Monroe
S. Callahan
I. Graves
Her breath caught.
Below that, freshly carved—sharper, cleaner, not yet worn by time:
N. Blackwell
Her knees buckled.

NORA
No... no, that wasn't there before.
The room whispered.
Not loud. Not screaming.

Just **enough.**
VOICES (OVERLAPPING)
Nora... you're already inside...
It doesn't want you to leave...
It wears your name now...
She turned, heart in her throat, flashlight beam dancing wildly.
The air shifted.
The whispers rose, now like water boiling under her skin.
VOICES (LOUDER)
Do you remember who you are?
Her hand gripped the locket at her neck.
It burned against her skin.
The whispers **stopped.**
Just like that.
Silence slammed into the room.
Then—
A breath behind her.
She turned.
The mirror on the far wall—cracked and dusted over—reflected **herself.**
But not **just** herself.
Her reflection **smiled.**
She hadn't.

REFLECTION (NORA'S VOICE)
It's easier if you forget. That's how she lost.
NORA
Who?
REFLECTION
Isadora. Me. You. All of us. Names fade. But the house stays full.*
The glass rippled.
Nora stumbled back, flashlight dropping with a clatter.

The room swelled with whispers again—faster now, desperate, all talking at once.

VOICES

Remember. Remember. REMEMBER.

She screamed.

And the room answered.

HALLWAY – MOMENTS LATER

Simon caught her as she stumbled out, eyes wild, hands bleeding where her nails had dug into her palms.

SIMON

What happened?

NORA

It has my name. My voice. My face. It's writing me **backwards.**

He stared at her.

SIMON

We have to stop it.

NORA

How? It's already inside. And if I forget who I am... what's left?

LIBRARY – NIGHT

She sat curled in the library chair again. The locket against her skin. The séance book on her lap.

She began to write her name in the margins of every page.

Over and over and over again.

Nora Blackwell. Nora Blackwell. Nora Blackwell.

Because the only thing more dangerous than a haunted house—

Was a house that wanted to become **you.**

CHAPTER 14
LOSING TIME

H OLLOW GRAVES – BASEMENT – 1892 (FLASHBACK)

THE RITUAL CIRCLE WAS WRONG.

She could feel it in her skin. It burned just beneath the surface, a fever she couldn't sweat out. The wax hadn't cooled properly. The blood hadn't dried. The soil wouldn't take it.

And yet Elijah continued.

He spoke the words from the séance book in a slow, rhythmic chant, one hand raised over the crib at the center of the room, the other holding the locket Isadora once wore around her neck.

He had stripped it from her like a surgeon removing a piece of skin.

ELIJAH
Let the voice speak. Let the veil thin. Let the house open.
Candles flickered violently.

The crib was empty.

It always was.

But tonight, it breathed.

A low sound—wheezing, rhythmic, wet—began to rise from the hollow beneath the stone floor. A heartbeat that wasn't hers. Not Elijah's. Not human.

Isadora stood at the edge of the circle, lips trembling.

ISADORA

You told me this was to silence the whispers.

ELIJAH

It is. But not by closing them.

He turned to her.

ELIJAH (CONT'D)

We must feed them what they want. They are hungry for memory, for grief, for the weight of the unspoken. You are perfect.

She shook her head.

ISADORA

You said I would bind it.

ELIJAH

You will. As its **anchor**. You will hold it here, with your sorrow, forever.

HOLLOW GRAVES – LIBRARY – PRESENT (NORA)

Nora woke with her head on the séance book, the fire still glowing beside her.

Had she fallen asleep?

No.

She hadn't even remembered closing her eyes.

The dream—

No.

The memory.

It was too real.

The stone floor. The circle. The crib. Elijah's voice.

Her fingers reached instinctively for the locket at her throat.
Still there.
Still warm.
She opened the séance book again.
The page she had never seen before was now marked with a smear of soot:
If the binding fails, the voice remains open.
The house learns the shape of the soul through repetition.
It becomes what it consumes.

BASEMENT STAIRWELL – MOMENTS LATER (NORA)
She descended the cellar stairs slowly, each creak of the wood loud enough to wake the dead.
The darkness below was not simply **absence of light**—it was **presence of something else.**
She carried no flashlight.
Only the locket.
At the bottom, the cellar opened like a wound—stone walls damp with age, air thick and sweet with rot.
She reached the back wall.
The place she'd seen in Isadora's memory.
And there—it waited.
The circle.
Charred into the stone. Ash still clinging to the edges, like blood that refused to fade.

BASEMENT – 1892 (ISADORA)
Isadora stepped backward as Elijah continued chanting, but her eyes were no longer on him.
They were on the **walls**.
They were **moving**.
Not visibly. Not like hands or shadows or ghosts.

But like the house was breathing through them.
And then—
A voice.
Not Elijah's.
Not hers.
Something older.
Something that sounded like *a thousand women whispering the same word at once.*
Isadora.
She screamed.
The circle flared with flame—and collapsed.
The candles blew out.
Elijah was gone.
And the crib—
The crib was full.

BASEMENT – PRESENT (NORA)

The circle flared.
Not flame—**memory.**
The room twisted around her. Her flashlight blinked back on—though she hadn't brought it. The cellar door closed itself above her with a deafening slam.
And then—
A mirror stood where the crib had been.
Cracked.
Inside it: **herself**, again.
Smiling.
But this time the reflection was older. Paler. Hollow-eyed.
Wearing Isadora's dress.

REFLECTION (NORA'S VOICE)
You already know how it ends.

NORA
Not this time.

She reached forward and **punched the mirror.**
It shattered like glass—and like sound.

LIBRARY – SECONDS LATER

She gasped awake.
Still on the couch.
The fire now dead.
Her hand was bleeding.
A shard of glass on the floor.
She had **never gone to the basement**.
And yet—her hand bled, exactly where she'd shattered the mirror.
The séance book lay open again.
This time, the final page had changed.
Time is not linear inside the Hollow.
The voice moves forward and backward.
She tried. You must finish it.
Nora stared at the page until the ink bled into tears.
Because she realized something.
She had seen the ritual fail from inside.
She hadn't dreamed Isadora's memory.
She had **been part of it.**

CHAPTER 15
FLASHBACK: RITUALS

Some rooms should never be found.
Some doors should never be noticed.
The nursery behind the mirror had been both.

HOLLOW GRAVES – UPSTAIRS CORRIDOR – EARLY MORNING
Nora had been walking the halls again.
Not pacing.
Not exploring.
Following.
The house was leading her. Or luring her. Or maybe it was just **echoing her thoughts back at her** until she forgot where they began.
This morning, the halls felt longer.
There were more doors than before.
More cracks in the wallpaper.
More shadows that held their breath.
And then she saw it—just past the old master bedroom, where a built-in bookshelf had always stood.

Except now, it was slightly ajar.
Books spilled at its base.
The wood swollen. Pushed out.
As though the wall itself was **exhaling**.
She stepped forward.
Behind the shelf, a **small wooden door**, the kind you'd find in a dollhouse.
Child-sized.
Painted sky blue, the color faded and chipped.
A brass knob shaped like a sleeping bird.
And carved, barely visible at the base:
NURSERY
She reached for the knob.
The moment her fingers touched it, the house sighed.

HIDDEN NURSERY – CONTINUOUS

The door opened on a room untouched by time.
Dustless.
Pristine.
Wrong.
A soft yellow glow filled the space, though there were no windows. A music box turned in slow, mechanical rhythm on a nightstand, playing a melody she remembered from her childhood—
Except she hadn't heard it before.
There were **six cribs**, arranged in a circle.
Inside each: a doll.
Not porcelain.
Not cloth.
Life-sized. Still. Dressed in burial gowns. Faces blank.
Nora stepped into the room and immediately felt the temperature drop.
She could **hear breathing**.
But not from the dolls.

From the walls.

She moved to the dresser and opened the top drawer.

Inside: **hair clippings**, labeled with initials.

I.G.

C.L.

E.M.

N.B.

Her fingers shook as she hovered over the last one. **N.B.** Her initials.

Except she had never been here before.

Right?

S HE TURNED SLOWLY toward the cribs again.

One of the dolls had **moved**.

Its head tilted toward her.

Its eyes were open.

Painted. But **aware.**

It smiled.

NORA (O.S.)

You've always been here.

She spun around.

Her own voice again.

But no one behind her.

The music box stopped.

A whisper began.

CHILDREN (OVERLAPPING)

Mama... mama... mama...

The voices layered over each other.

Not playful.

Not innocent.

Desperate.

She backed out of the nursery and slammed the door shut.

It didn't click.

It **breathed.**

PARLOR – HOURS LATER
The fire had been dead for some time, but she hadn't noticed. Nora sat on the rug, arms wrapped around her knees, staring at the doorway.
She didn't know how long she'd been there.
Maybe minutes.
Maybe hours.
Time no longer played fair in this house.
Then—
Footsteps.
She turned toward the front door just as it creaked open.
Simon.
He stood in the threshold, soaked with rain, pale, hollow-eyed.
NORA
Simon?
He smiled.
But it was too wide.
Too slow.
SIMON
I found what we need.
He stepped inside.
The air around him seemed to **tighten.**
Nora didn't move.
She watched his eyes.
They looked like his.
They sounded like his.
But they didn't **feel** like him.
He set a leather-bound book on the table.
Same paper as the séance text.
It smelled of dirt and old blood.
SIMON (CONT'D)

It told me the last name. The one that finishes it.

She stared at the book.

Her skin prickled.

NORA

Where did you find this?

He tilted his head.

SIMON

You showed me.

And then, softly:

SIMON (CONT'D)

Don't you remember?

CHAPTER 16
THE ONES WHO HELPED BURY HER

He smelled like rain and old wood.
 But something underneath that.
 Like he'd been **sleeping underground**.

PARLOR – NIGHT

Simon sat across from her at the long oak table. The storm pressed against the windows in waves, thunder rolling through the walls like a warning.

He poured tea from a kettle she didn't remember boiling.

Nora watched him carefully.

His movements were... deliberate. Too careful. Like someone pretending to be familiar with their own skin.

SIMON
You haven't said much.

NORA
Neither have you.

He looked up, smiled softly.

SIMON

You're scared of me.

Not a question.

NORA

I don't know what you are.

A beat.

He blinked slowly, like something rebooting.

SIMON

I'm the same. Just... tired. I walked all night.

NORA

And found a ritual book buried under a tree, bound in skin?

His smile faltered.

He reached into his coat and pulled out an envelope—faded, brittle with age. Set it on the table.

Nora hesitated. Opened it.

Inside: **a photograph.**

A staff photo. Taken outside Hollow Graves in 1892.

There, standing beside Elijah Graves, was a man who looked **exactly like Simon.**

Same sharp jaw. Same haunted eyes.

On the back of the photo, in tight script:

W. Ward – Record Keeper, 1891–1893

Assisted in final silence. Loyal to the end.

Her blood ran cold.

NORA

You knew.

He didn't deny it.

SIMON

I didn't want to believe it. My father never spoke about him. Just called him the reason the town kept its mouth shut.

NORA

You're not just connected to this house. Your family helped it.

SIMON

Not me.

NORA

How do I know that?

The lights flickered.

The fireplace hissed.

The house was listening.

LIBRARY – LATER THAT NIGHT

Nora retreated to the library, ritual book in hand. She didn't want to sleep. Not with Simon in the house.

She flipped through the pages, fingers trembling.

Each section was older than the last. Layers of handwriting. Updates. Bloodstains.

And finally—near the back—she found it.

A line written in the margin, next to a page on mimicry:

When the house cannot break you, it replaces you.

It starts with the ones you trust.

She slammed the book shut.

Outside the door, footsteps.

Soft.

Measured.

Not approaching. Not retreating.

Just **waiting**.

INT. SIMON'S ROOM – MIDNIGHT

Nora opened his door.

He was asleep.

Or pretending.

She crossed the room silently.

A journal sat on his desk.

Not ancient. Not ritualistic.

Modern.

She opened it.

The first few pages: notes about Hollow Graves. Drawings of symbols. Mentions of Isadora.

Then the entries changed.
Nora doesn't remember the door that moves. But I do.
She repeats things now. Words she's never said.
The house is copying her—or she's copying it.
I can't tell anymore.
And the last entry, dated **yesterday**:
If I don't come back the same, I hope she knows how to tell the difference.

LIBRARY – DAWN

She sat beside the cold hearth, the locket wrapped tightly in her hand, reading that entry again.

Tears welled, unbidden.

Because maybe Simon was telling the truth.

Maybe he knew what the house would try.

Maybe this wasn't him.

Or maybe it was.

And it didn't matter.

Because now, the house had a copy of both of them.

And it was getting **better** at pretending.

INT. NURSERY – SAME TIME

The dolls in the cribs had shifted.

One had turned its head toward the door.

Another had moved its hand to its chest.

And the one in the center—dressed like Isadora—opened its glassy eyes and whispered:

DOLL (ISADORA'S VOICE)
He is not the one who returns. He is the one who lets it in.

CHAPTER 17
THINGS THAT SHOULDN'T CHANGE BUT DO

Doors don't move.

Not in the real world.

Not unless someone opens them, closes them, rips them from the hinges.

But this door—

This door had simply **disappeared.**

SECOND FLOOR LANDING – EARLY MORNING

Nora stood in front of where her bedroom door had been for the past three weeks.

The wall was seamless now.

Same faded wallpaper.

Same crack running down the side.

No frame. No knob. No sign it had ever existed.

Her room was gone.

She pressed her hand to the wall.

It was cold. Solid. Completely unyielding.

Her breath stuttered.

She looked down the hall. Every door was there—just as before.

Except hers.

And Simon's.

She ran to his.

Same result.

Seamless wall.

Gone.

FOYER – MOMENTS LATER

She rushed down the stairs, barefoot, heartbeat stuttering in her ears.

SIMON!

No answer.

Not from the parlor.

Not from the kitchen.

Not from anywhere.

She opened the front door.

Fog.

Thick. Yellow-gray. Smelling faintly of turned earth and something sweet—like bruised fruit left too long in the sun.

The yard was gone. The road. The tree line.

Everything swallowed by the mist.

She stepped outside. Her foot hit dirt. But the fog refused to part. Sound vanished in it. Her own voice was dampened.

NORA

Simon?

A whisper answered.

But it came from **inside the house**.

She turned.

The door had closed.

HOLLOW GRAVES – ENTRANCE HALL – CONTINUOUS

She grabbed the handle.

Twisted.

Locked.

From the inside.

She pounded on it.

Nothing.

Then—

A soft sound behind her.

A creak. A sigh. A thud. A familiar rhythm.

Simon's footsteps.

She turned, relief flaring in her chest—

But the hallway was **empty**.

Then she saw it.

The staircase to the second floor now **split in two**, winding in opposite directions like a spiral. The wallpaper had changed. Different pattern. Different decade.

The air was colder.

She turned in a slow circle, heart racing.

The **house was rearranging itself.**

LIBRARY – MINUTES OR HOURS LATER

Time blurred.

She wasn't sure how she got there.

Books had fallen off shelves that hadn't existed before.

The windows were bricked up now.

One page of the séance book lay open on the floor, soaking up spilled ink from a bottle she didn't remember knocking over.

The text blurred and shifted like heat mirage.

She tried to read it.

Tried to hold a thought.

But everything in her mind kept looping back to one word:

Unreal.

And then—

From behind her—

SIMON (O.S.)

You shouldn't be here.

She turned.

He was in the doorway.

Soaked. Pale.

Same clothes. Same expression.

NORA

You left.

SIMON

Did I?

NORA

You were gone. Your room is gone.

SIMON

Maybe you left.

He stepped forward.

SIMON (CONT'D)

Maybe it's been you all along.

Her back hit the bookshelf.

She stared into his eyes.

They were his.

But the warmth behind them?

Gone.

NORA

What did the house show you?

He smiled, slow and crooked.

SIMON

Everything.

NURSERY – SAME TIME

The dolls had moved again.

Now they were **sitting upright** in their cribs.

Hands folded.
Heads tilted.
Waiting.
One had Nora's hair. Same locket. Same freckles.
It blinked once.
And then began to hum.

HOLLOW GRAVES – LATER (UNKNOWN TIME)

Nora sat in the hallway.

The walls were pulsing, soft and warm like something alive.

Her hands were stained with ink, but she didn't know what she'd written.

She touched her face.

It didn't feel like her own.

The house had removed her room, her sense of time, her sense of direction.

All she had left was a question:

What happens when the house finishes its version of you?

CHAPTER 18
THE PLACE WHERE NAMES GO TO DIE

The house was quiet now.
    And that was worse than when it screamed.

HOLLOW GRAVES MANOR – PARLOR – NIGHT
    Nora sat in the parlor, surrounded by open books and burnt pages, her back to the cold hearth.
    She hadn't seen Simon in hours.
    Or maybe days.
    Time wasn't something she could trust anymore. Not the mirrors. Not the walls. Not even her reflection.
    But one thing remained constant.
    The **voice** in the locket.
    It was faint. Gentle.
    Isadora.
    Sometimes crying.
    Sometimes humming.
    But tonight, it spoke:

ISADORA (V.O.)

You're almost there. You must finish what I began. Or the house will finish you.

Nora didn't answer aloud.

She was afraid her voice no longer belonged to her.

INT. SECOND FLOOR – WHISPERING ROOM – LATER

She returned to the room she once swore she'd never enter again.

The Whispering Room was darker now. The names on the walls had begun to **bleed**.

Not ink. Not blood.

But **memory.**

She saw flashes as she passed each one.

• A woman rocking an empty cradle.

• Another, screaming inside a locked closet.

• Another, burning her journal page by page, whispering, *they're watching from the floorboards.*

And finally—

Her name.

Carved deeper than before.

N. BLACKWELL

Underneath it, new words had appeared:

You were always meant to come home.

She ran her thumb across them.

The wall shuddered.

A section fell open, revealing **stairs.**

Leading down.

RITUAL CHAMBER – BELOW THE HOUSE

The air changed.

Thicker. Warmer. Damp.

Like she'd entered the belly of a living thing.

The chamber was circular. The walls were carved with runes she recognized from the séance book, but here—they pulsed faintly.

The ritual circle was redrawn. Fresh. Waiting.

And at its center:

A **mirror**.

Not broken.

Not cracked.

But **alive**.

The surface shimmered like mercury. And inside it—

Nora saw herself.

Only older.

Palest skin.

Eyes blackened.

Mouth stitched shut.

A creature half-remembered, half-becoming.

The mirror-Nora reached forward.

MIRROR-NORA

We bind or we become.

CHAMBER – MOMENTS LATER

Nora knelt at the circle.

The ritual book in front of her. The locket beside it.

She read Isadora's final journal page—left beneath the book.

Elijah thought sacrifice was silence. He was wrong.

The only way to bind it is to speak the names it has stolen.

To say them aloud. To remember what it tried to erase.

She looked at the wall.

Thousands of names.

Some carved by hand.

Others by suffering.

She picked up the locket.

Held it to her lips.

And began to speak.

One name. Then another.
E. Monroe. C. Lancaster. I. Graves. N. Blackwell.
The room shook.
The walls bled light.
The mirror began to scream.
But it was her scream.

HOUSE – SIMULTANEOUS
In the attic, the dolls began to burn.
In the Whispering Room, the names began to glow.
In the nursery, the cribs turned to ash.
And the house—
The house **howled.**
It wasn't made to be remembered.
It was made to contain what the world didn't want to see.
But Nora?
She **remembered everything.**

RITUAL CHAMBER – FINAL MOMENTS
The locket cracked in her hand.
The mirror shattered—not with sound, but **with silence** so complete it knocked her to the floor.
The circle flashed once.
Then extinguished.
Nora lay on the stone, blinking up at nothing.
And for the first time since she arrived—
She heard **only her own breath.**

CHAPTER 19
THE LAST TRICK OF THE HOUSE

RITUAL CHAMBER – EARLY MORNING
Nora lay on the stone floor.
The circle was gone. The mirror: shattered. The locket: ash in her palm.

Silence reigned.

Real silence.

No voices. No whispers. No mimicry.

She sat up slowly, the light from above now soft—real sunlight.

It had never reached this deep before.

Her body ached. Her throat burned. But she remembered every name.

And for the first time since arriving…

She knew who she was.

SECOND FLOOR – HALLWAY – LATER
She climbed the stairs.

The house groaned, but not with hunger. With **collapse**.

Cracks split the floorboards. Wallpaper peeled like old scabs.

Light bled through places it shouldn't—like the house had lost the strength to hold itself together.

She passed the nursery door.

It was open.

Inside: **empty cribs.**

No dolls.

Just scattered hair ribbons and melted wax.

She kept walking.

MASTER BEDROOM – DAYLIGHT

She stepped into the master bedroom.

Clean. Quiet. Drenched in morning sun.

The bed made.

The windows open.

And there—

Sitting in the chair by the window—**Simon.**

Not pale. Not twisted. Not wrong.

Just… him.

He looked up. Smiled.

SIMON

You did it.

She stared at him.

Every instinct screamed to run.

But something in her heart whispered: *Wait.*

NORA

Did I?

SIMON

The house is quiet now. Isn't that enough?

She stepped closer.

Watched his eyes.

SIMON (CONT'D)

We can leave. The fog is gone. You don't have to carry this anymore.

She blinked.
SIMON (CONT'D)
You could stay. Write the book. Tell the story. Make her death mean something.
A pause.
SIMON (CONT'D)
Or you could forget. Like everyone else did.
That broke the spell.
NORA
You were doing so well until then.
The smile faltered.
SIMON (CONT'D)
She didn't want to be remembered, you know. That's why she left the door open.
NORA
No. She left it open for me.
The thing wearing Simon's face tilted its head.
The sunlight flickered. Once. Twice.
Then died.
The windows slammed shut.
The room went black.

REFLECTION ROOM – MOMENTS LATER
She was standing in a room of mirrors.
Dozens.
Each one showing a different version of her.
Screaming. Crying. Bleeding. Smiling.
One laughing.
One still.
Which was real?
The house whispered—
HOUSE (V.O.)

You are every memory you've lost. Every silence you survived. Every lie you told yourself to get through the night.

One mirror shattered.

Then another.

Then another.

Until only one was left.

And inside it—

Isadora.

Smiling. Calm.

She pressed a hand to the glass.

ISADORA

Finish it.

Nora pressed her hand to hers.

FOYER – FINAL MOMENTS

She walked to the front door.

It was unlocked.

The fog was gone.

Sunlight spilled across the threshold like blessing.

She looked back.

The house creaked behind her—timber groaning under weight long carried.

And from deep within the walls, the **whispers returned**.

But only one.

One voice.

ISADORA (V.O.)

Don't forget us.

Nora stepped outside.

And **didn't look back.**

EPILOGUE – THE HOUSE THAT WASN'T SILENT ANYMORE

The house was gone.
At least, that's what the papers said.
A fire. A storm. A freak accident during renovations. "Historic Victorian manor collapses under its own weight after decades of neglect."

No mention of rituals. No mention of Isadora Graves.
No mention of the hundreds of names carved into the walls.
Just silence.
Again.
But Nora had learned what silence meant in a house like that.
It meant someone had rewritten the ending.
She would not let them do it again.

NORA'S APARTMENT – PRESENT DAY

The room was small. Simple. Clean. Windows open to a gray, quiet morning. There was coffee cooling on the desk, a half-burned candle nearby, and her laptop blinking with a cursor waiting on the title page:

The House of Hollow Graves
by Nora Blackwell

Her fingers hovered over the keyboard.

She had written the prologue four times. Deleted it six. Restarted once after waking from a dream where her reflection smiled without her.

But this time—this morning—she didn't begin with the house.

She began with **a name**.

Isadora Graves was not mad. She was not a myth. She was not the villain in her husband's story.

She was the first to fight back.

FLASHBACK – ISADORA'S FINAL MEMORY

She stands in the ritual circle, candlelight behind her.

Alone. Afraid. But steady.

Elijah is gone. The others gone before her. But she remains.

She presses her palm to the floor.

Blood seeps into the stone.

And in a whisper:

ISADORA

Let this truth live longer than me.

NORA'S APARTMENT – CONTINUOUS

Nora wiped her eyes, not out of sadness—but reverence.

She wrote her way through the pain.

Through the names.

She told their stories.

Each woman. Each whisper.

She didn't flinch from the horror of it—because that's what Hollow Graves wanted: to be beautiful, silent, forgotten.

But silence was not protection.

It was a **prison**.

. . .

BOOKSTORE – MONTHS LATER
The hardcover sat in the window display.
THE HOUSE OF HOLLOW GRAVES
A gothic memoir of inherited silence, haunting, and the women history tried to erase.
It sold quietly at first. Then loudly.
Then, endlessly.
People read it. Believed it. Shared it.
And when they closed the final page, they did not forget Isadora's name.

RADIO INTERVIEW – ONE YEAR LATER
A host leaned across the microphone.
HOST
There's a rumor you made it all up. That Hollow Graves never existed.
Nora smiled.
NORA
Good. Let them think that.
HOST
Why?
She paused.
Looked directly into the recording light.
NORA
Because the house can't find new voices if it doesn't hear its name anymore.
A beat.
NORA (CONT'D)
But just in case—
She opened her hand.
Inside: a matchbook.

From **The Silver Gull**, the diner in Ashvale.
She set it on the table.
The camera caught the flash of the address.

NORA'S BEDROOM – NIGHT
She sat up in bed, staring at the ceiling.
Outside, wind rustled the leaves.
Inside, the world was quiet.
But sometimes, in the very stillness between heartbeats, she could almost hear:
Thank you.
A whisper.
Her name.
Not her own.
But one she would never forget.
Isadora.
She whispered it aloud.
Once more.
Just to keep her real.

There is always a last
house at the end of the road.
Always a gate that shouldn't
open. Always a voice that
sounds like yours.

When you hear it...

Don't answer.

Unless you're ready to become
part of the story.

(The door is still there.)

Discovered folded behind the last page of the original manuscript. Origin unknown.

Afterword: From the Journal of Isadora Graves

From the Journal of Isadora Graves
(*Found hidden beneath the third floor hearthstone—unburned, untouched.*)

To the one who heard me—

I don't know your name.

But I know your voice.

I know the way your breath caught the first time you saw your own reflection smile without you. I know the weight in your spine when a floorboard creaked and you *knew* it wasn't just the house settling. I know what it feels like to write a warning in a place no one will ever read and pray—**just once**—that a single word survives.

You heard me.

That was enough.

I wanted so badly to be the ending. To close the door. To bind the silence so no one else had to carry it. But the truth is, it needed a name stronger than mine. It needed yours.

Let them call you survivor. Let them say you imagined it. Let them turn away from the truth with closed mouths and quiet eyes. But don't you ever stop speaking.

AFTERWORD: FROM THE JOURNAL OF ISADORA GRAVES

Don't stop saying names.
That's how we live.
That's how the walls stay empty.
Yours in shadow and memory,

Isadora

Acknowledgments

Writing this novel was like walking through a mirror and leaving a little piece of myself behind. I never expected the ghosts to follow me out.

To those who have loved a good haunted house story—not just for the shivers, but for the silence inside it—you were my people long before I ever put pen to page.

To the gothic giants: Shirley Jackson, Daphne du Maurier, Toni Morrison, and Silvia Moreno-Garcia—you taught me that haunted isn't always horror, and horror isn't always what knocks.

To the survivors: the ones who whisper their truths because shouting would be too painful. You are brave in ways the world doesn't understand.

To my early readers (you know who you are): thank you for letting me walk you through the halls of Hollow Graves before the wallpaper even curled.

And to the one who left the door open—

I don't know if I found you in the story, or if you found me.

But you are remembered now.

Rowan Hale

www.ingramcontent.com/pod-product-compliance
Lightning Source LLC
LaVergne TN
LVHW050024080526
838202LV00069B/6909